The Thing in the Cave

by Dina Anastasio
illustrated by Lyn Boyer

Jamal's Secret

by Amanda Jenkins
illustrated by Shawn Byous

TWO REALISTIC FICTION STORIES

Table of Contents

Realistic Fiction

What is realistic fiction?

Realistic fiction features characters and plots that could actually happen in everyday life. The settings are authentic—they are based on familiar places such as a home, school, office, or farm. The stories involve some type of conflict, or problem. The conflict can be something a character faces within himself, an issue between characters, or a problem between a character and nature.

What is the purpose of realistic fiction?

Realistic fiction shows how people grow and learn, deal with successes and failures, make decisions, build relationships, and solve problems. In addition to making readers think and wonder, realistic fiction is entertaining. Most of us enjoy "escaping" into someone else's life for a while.

How do you read realistic fiction?

First, note the title. The title will give you a clue about an important character or conflict in the story. As you read, pay attention to the thoughts, feelings, and actions of the main characters. Note how the characters change from the beginning of the story to the end. Ask yourself: *What moves this character to action? Can I learn something from his or her struggles?*

Features of

Realistic Fiction

The story takes place in an authentic setting.

At least one character deals with a conflict (self, others, or nature).

The characters are like people you might meet in real life.

The story is told from a first-person or third-person point of view.

Who tells the story in realistic fiction?

Authors usually write realistic fiction in one of two ways. In the first-person point of view, one of the characters tells the story as it happens to him or her, using words such as **I**, **me**, **my**, **mine**, **we**, **us**, and **our**. In the third-person point of view, a narrator tells the story, using words such as **he**, **she**, **they**, **their**, and the proper names of the characters.

Meet the Characters

Cave Adventures

Summer has finally arrived. Linda and her brother Jake have been coming to the same cabin on this rocky beach since they were little. Their friend Maria is back for her second summer. Cai is new to the seacoast. This summer promises new adventures since Linda and Jake's dad recently discovered a hidden cave.

Linda, 12, is a big talker with big ideas. She loves technology and gadgets, and hates that the cabins do not get TV reception or the Internet.

Jake, 11, is a smart boy who enjoys playing tricks and shooting hoops on the basket outside the cabin.

Maria, 10, is an only child. She lives with her divorced mother. She likes to bake and cook, and usually has her nose in a book.

Cai, 11, is spending the summer with his grandma. He likes to swim, fish, and play with his dog Tucker.

Oak Street Kids

Five kids couldn't be more different than Jalissa, Jamal, Brooke, Luke, and Tia. But they have some things in common, too! They all live in the Oak Street Apartments. They all have parents who work during the day. They are in the same afterschool "club" run by the manager of the apartment building, Ms. Tilly. That's why the Oak Street Kids have made a deal: They will always stick together and help one another.

Jalissa, 10, likes drama and excitement, and is Jamal's twin sister.

Jamal, 10, is calm and easygoing, the opposite of his twin sister.

Brooke, 11, can always be counted on to organize and take charge.

Luke, 11, may not be a top student, but he's loyal and fun.

Tia, 9, loves every kind of sport.

Ms. Tilly is the no-nonsense manager of the Oak Street Apartments and takes care of the kids after school.

The Thing in the Cave

"Tucker! Where are you? Come home, boy!" Tucker is my dog. He's a Jack Russell terrier. When he's not eating, there's nothing he likes better than chasing birds.

Here's what happened: We were sitting on our cabin steps, staring out at the waves. "What should we do," I asked, "for today, and the next six weeks?" Then a seagull swooped down onto the sand. It stood there like a statue, watching us.

Tucker's ears perked up. He barked a few times, but the gull didn't move. Tucker barked again, and then took off after the gull.

I thought he'd stop running and barking as soon as the gull was in the air. But my dog kept right on chasing the gull down the beach until I couldn't see him anymore, and that got me worried.

I was **concerned** because Tucker and I had only been at the beach for one day. Would he be able to find his way back to Granny's cabin? I certainly didn't want to lose my only friend on the first day of summer vacation.

I walked a little way down the sand. I saw a red-haired boy building a sand castle. I asked if he had seen a Jack Russell terrier chasing a gull. He said he hadn't seen any dogs. Then he asked if I'd like to help with the castle.

"Later," I said. "I have to find my dog now."

"My name is Jake," the boy said as he scooped some sand from the moat.

"I'm Cai," I told him as I looked around for Tucker.

A little farther down the beach, a dark-haired girl was reading a book. She said her name was Maria.

"No, I haven't seen any dogs," she said. "Then again, this book is so good that I haven't looked up for a long time."

I was telling Maria about Tucker when another girl raced down the beach **hollering** Jake's name. Then she started shouting Maria's name. She was so excited that she stepped right on Jake's castle. The turrets caved in. The walls buckled and then **collapsed** into the moat like melting snowmen.

"I'll get you for this, Linda!" Jake screamed. He stood up and glared at his sister. Linda didn't seem to care at all. She didn't even say that she was sorry. She was looking off into the distance.

"Follow me!" she ordered. "Dad discovered a cave!"

Everyone lined up behind Linda, like ducklings following their mother. I joined the tail end of the line. As we marched toward the cave, I kept calling, "Tucker! Tucker!"

Within two minutes, we were at the cave. One by one, we peeked inside. But no one went in. Not even Linda. Maria wondered if there were any stalactites and stalagmites hanging from the ceiling or growing from the floor, but she didn't go in to see.

"Check it out!" Linda told Jake.

"Who says?" Jake asked huffily as he folded his arms.

"I do!" Linda commanded, and Jake went in.

"Now you!" Linda pointed at Maria. The smaller girl pushed the glasses up her nose. She was as calm as a well-fed old cat. She just shrugged and strolled in like she didn't have a care in the world.

Linda and I stood by the cave opening and listened. At first we heard Jake and Maria whispering and **murmuring**. Then we heard nothing at all. I glanced over at Linda. She was staring at me like she was waiting for something. I knew what she was waiting for. In about ten seconds, she was going to order me into the cave. Normally that wouldn't have bothered me, because I'm always up for an adventure. But I had something more important to do. I had to find Tucker.

"Well?" Linda said.

"Well what?"

"You should be in there."

"You should go first," I suggested politely. "Be my guest."

Linda took a few steps backward, away from the cave opening. "I'll go later," she shrugged. She drew a circle in the sand with the toe of her shoe.

I suddenly realized what was happening. Linda was afraid to go into the cave! Maybe she thought that if she *sounded* tough and brave, we'd think that she *was* tough and brave.

We listened for a little longer, and then I called to Jake and Maria. We heard nothing. "We better look for them. I'll go in with you," I suggested.

Linda shook her head, took another step back, and said, "You go."

"What are you scared of?" I asked.

She hesitated and then told me. Her words came out fast. She was nervous. "I'm afraid of the dark. Maybe there's a monster in there."

"I don't think so," I said, taking her hand.

I led Linda inside. It was dark in there—too dark to see Maria or Jake or anything else.

That's when I heard the sound. Something was breathing hard. At first I thought it was Jake trying to frighten us. Maybe he was trying to pay Linda back for ruining his castle.

I listened carefully. Then I realized that I had been wrong. The breathing was more like a loud steady

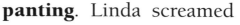

panting. Linda screamed "Monster!" which made me jump about a foot. She pulled free of my hand and raced outside. When she was gone, Jake tapped my shoulder and whispered my name.

"What?" I whispered back.

"What's making that noise?" Jake sounded nervous.

"I don't know," said Maria. "And I'm not planning on finding out!" She quickly crawled backward out of the cave so as not to upset The Thing. Jake followed her into the daylight.

11

I was alone in the cave with The Thing, but I wasn't afraid. I had heard that panting sound many, many times before.

I whistled once. The panting stopped. I whistled again and Tucker whimpered and whined softly. I whistled a third time and he ran to me. I leaned down and petted him. He barked loudly, over and over. The barks echoed off the walls of the cave, bouncing back and forth.

When he was finished barking, Tucker jumped into my arms and licked my face. I carried him outside for the others to see.

"Ladies and gentleman," I said. "Meet The Thing, also known as my dog, Tucker."

Reread the Story

Analyze the Characters, Setting, and Plot
- Who were the characters in the story?
- Where and when does the story take place?
- Which character is telling the story?
- What was the main character's problem?
- What do you think might happen after the kids meet Tucker?

Analyze the Tools Writers Use: Simile
- On page 6, the author says a seagull "stood there like a statue." Was the seagull moving? Standing still?
- On page 8, the author says the castle walls collapsed "like melting snowmen." Do you think the walls melted slowly or quickly? Explain.
- On page 9, the author says Maria was "as calm as a well-fed old cat" and strolled into the cave. Was Maria frightened or not? Explain.

Focus on Words: Synonyms
Synonyms are words that have a similar meaning.
For example, in this story **whimpered** and **whined** are synonyms that mean "cried softly." Make a chart like the one below. Then reread the story to find synonyms for the following words.

Page	Word	Synonym	How do you know?
7	concerned		
8	hollering		
8	collapsed		
9	murmuring		
11	panting		

Jamal's Secret

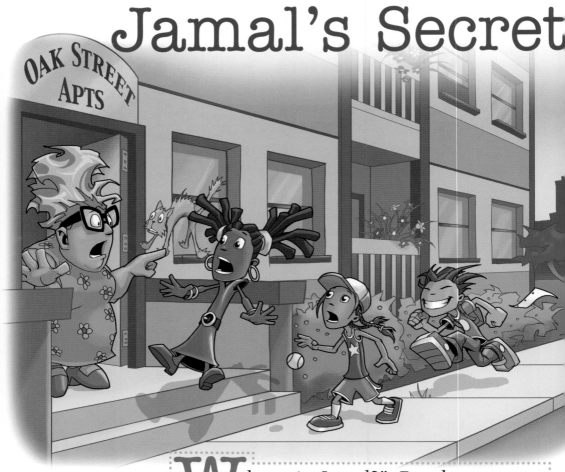

The author uses the third-person point of view. She gives the setting in the beginning of the story. The Oak Street Apartments is a place that could actually exist. This lets the reader know that the story is realistic fiction.

W here is Jamal?" Brooke wondered one day after school. She and the other kids from the Oak Street Apartments always walked home together. But today, Jamal was nowhere in sight.

"Maybe he got in trouble and had to stay after school," said Luke.

"Jamal is not like *you*, Luke," said Jalissa. "He doesn't get in trouble, even by accident. Maybe he was kidnapped by aliens!"

"Yeah, right. Or maybe he already went home," suggested Tia, bouncing a tennis ball on the sidewalk. "We should go ask Ms. Tilly."

Crabby Ms. Tilly was the manager of the Oak Street Apartments. She also took care of the kids after school. They were a little afraid of her because she was so grumpy and strict.

When they got to the Oak Street Apartments, Jalissa flung the door open. She rushed inside, almost knocking Ms. Tilly down. "Jamal has been kidnapped by aliens!" she announced dramatically.

"Watch where you're going," scolded Ms. Tilly, "and don't bang the door. And Tia, stop bouncing that ball!"

"Excuse me, Ms. Tilly," Brooke asked politely. "Have you seen Jamal?"

"He got here five minutes ago," answered Ms. Tilly. "He's doing laundry."

"Laundry?" Luke echoed, surprised.

"Yes, he just took a load of towels down to the basement."

The author establishes the different personalities of the main characters with their dialogue and with descriptions of their actions.

The reader can tell this is a realistic story because the main characters are like kids you might know. They hang out together, understand one another's personalities, tease one another, and worry about one another.

15

Jamal doing laundry? The kids had to see this. They trooped down to the basement. When Jamal saw them, he quickly turned off the light.

"What are you hiding, Jamal?" called Luke.

"N-nothing," said Jamal.

But in one corner of the unlit basement, two eyes glowed red. In the dark the kids could make out a shadowy creature almost as large as the washing machine. It was growling.

"What is that?" cried Brooke.

"An alien!" said Jalissa.

"The bogeyman!" said Tia.

"A mad cow!" said Luke.

"It's a dog," Jamal said, and he turned on the light.

A big dog with a huge jaw glared at them from the corner. Its sagging jowls barely covered teeth as sharp as a wolf's fangs.

"I'm thinking of naming him Muffin," said Jamal.

"Muffin?" shrieked Jalissa. "That's a T-Rex!"

"Aw, he's nice," Jamal protested. "He almost got hit by a car. I found him trembling on the sidewalk, and brought him here. He hasn't had anything to eat in a long time—look how skinny he is!"

"We can tell he hasn't had anything to eat," said Luke. "He's looking at us like we're raw meat he's about to swallow in one gulp."

The author uses a simile to show Luke's fear, and also his sense of humor.

"Ms. Tilly won't let you keep that dog," warned Brooke.

"Yes she will," Jamal insisted. "My mom asked her if I could have a dog. Ms. Tilly said yes, if I took proper care of it."

"Mom asked if you could have a little dog," Jalissa corrected.

The author presents the problem of the story. It is a conflict between one character and another. Will Ms. Tilly let Jamal keep the dog?

"That's not a dog at all," said Luke. "That's a fur mountain with teeth."

"Come on," Jamal begged his friends. "Help me get him cleaned up before Ms. Tilly sees him . . . please?"

Of course, they agreed to help. The kids of the Oak Street Apartments always stuck together. Brooke, as usual, took charge. "Luke, hook up the hose. Jamal, get the towels ready. Jalissa and Tia, start filling that tub. I'll go get some soap."

The author develops the story by having the characters work together to help their friend Jamal. The author also reveals more about the characters' personalities through their actions and dialogue.

When Brooke returned with the soap, she was also wearing a raincoat, a rain hat, and rubber gloves.

"It's a dog bath, not a hurricane," Luke said, laughing.

"I'm not touching that animal unless there are layers between me and his **filth**," Brooke said. "Just look at all that dirt! Now, how are we going to get him into the tub?"

"Get in the tub, boy!" Jamal said hopefully.

The dog barked at Jamal. It probably meant to say "Woof! Woof!" but the sound was muffled by its **drooping** jowls. What came out instead was, "Bff! Bff!"

Then, surprisingly, the dog got into the tub. "A dog that likes to bathe? I think he really *is* an alien," said Jalissa.

The kids went to work. Luke ran the hose. Brooke was in charge of the soap. Jalissa, Tia, and Jamal scrubbed at various dog parts. Everything was going fine . . . until the dog decided it didn't like being wet. From head to tail it shook, flinging dirt, soapsuds, and water on the floor, the walls, and the five kids.

"Gross!" Brooke shouted as she ducked her head. Luke let go, and Jalissa and Tia jumped back. Jamal tried to hang on, but one person was not enough to hold a dog the size of a refrigerator. The dog broke free and ran.

All five kids ran after him, slipping and **skidding** in his trail of muddy suds. They were right behind him as he ran up the stairs.

When dog and kids reached the top, Ms. Tilly was coming down the hall. Her eyes bugged out when she saw the wet beast leap at her. She threw up her hands and screamed, "AUGH!"

The author makes the problem grow worse. The big, wet dog jumps on Ms. Tilly. The reader is left wondering what she will do. Will she let Jamal keep this dog?

The dog stopped short. Ms. Tilly's frightened scream seemed to have broken his heart. He collapsed like a limp noodle and rolled onto his back. With a pleading look, he put one paw up, asking Ms. Tilly for forgiveness.

Ms. Tilly touched the dog's outstretched paw. "Why, you're just a big sweetie," she told him.

"Bff?" the dog asked Ms. Tilly.

"And your name is Buff?" Ms. Tilly asked with an odd cooing sound.

"Bff!" agreed the dog, and he sat up.

Ms. Tilly turned to Jamal and demanded, "Is this the dog you asked about? He's **gigantic**!"

"Y-yes," said Jamal. "I know he's big, but . . ."

"Humph!" said Ms. Tilly. "Little dogs are yappy and annoying and remind me of rats. I prefer big dogs— the bigger the better!"

"You mean I can keep him?"

"Yes, Jamal," Ms. Tilly said softly. Then at her usual volume she blasted, "Now get this mess cleaned up!"

The problem has a happy solution! The author surprises the reader by making Ms. Tilly tough but with a soft spot for big dogs. The main character learns that other people aren't always what they seem. The author leaves the reader with the same message.

The kids herded Buff back to the basement. "This has taught me a lesson," Jamal remarked as they finished giving Buff his bath. "Even the scariest creature may have a secret soft side."

"Yeah," Luke agreed. "Buff is a pretty cool dog."

"I don't mean Buff," said Jamal. "I mean Ms. Tilly!"

20

Analyze the Characters, Setting, and Plot
- Who were the characters in the story?
- Where and when does the story take place?
- Is the story written in first-person point of view or third-person point of view? How do you know?
- What was the main character's problem?
- What relationships does the main character have with other characters? How do those relationships affect the outcome of the story?

Analyze the Tools Writers Use: Simile
- On page 16, the author says the shadowy creature was "as large as the washing machine." Why does the author make this comparison?
- On page 16, the author says the dog's teeth were "as sharp as a wolf's fangs." What is the author trying to tell the readers?
- On page 19, the author says the dog collapsed "like a limp noodle." Does this action make you think the dog is dangerous or not? Explain.

Focus on Words: Synonyms
Make a chart like the one below. Then look for synonyms in the story to help you understand each word.

Page	Word	Synonym	How do you know?
15	crabby		
18	filth		
18	drooping		
19	skidding		
19	gigantic		

How does an author write

Realistic Fiction?

Reread "Jamal's Secret" and think about what Amanda Jenkins did to write this story. How did she develop it? How can you, as a writer, develop your own story?

1. Decide on a Problem

Remember: The characters in realistic fiction face the same problems that you might face. In "Jamal's Secret," the problem is that a boy wants a dog but the building manager might not let him keep the dog he rescues.

Character	Jamal	Brooke	Ms. Tilly
Traits	kind; determined	worrier; organized	cranky; soft-hearted
Examples	He takes good care of a frightened dog. He wants to clean up the dog so Ms. Tilly will let him keep it.	She wants to know what happened to Jamal, and then she takes charge of how to help him.	She's full of rules and demands, but she coos at the dog and calls him a sweetie.

2. Brainstorm Characters
Writers ask these questions:

- What kind of person will my main character be? What are his or her traits? Interests?

- What things are important to my main character? What does he or she want?

- What other characters will be important to my story? How will each one help or hinder the main character?

- How will the characters change? What will they learn about life?

3. Brainstorm Setting and Plot
Writers ask these questions:

- Where does my story take place? How will I describe the setting?

- What is the problem, or situation?

- What events happen? How does the story end?

- Will my readers be entertained? Will they learn something?

Setting	Oak Street Apartments
Problem of the Story	A boy has found a large stray dog. He wants to keep it, but he's not sure if the cranky building manager will let him.
Story Events	1. The boy's friends help him clean up the dog. 2. The dog runs off and encounters the manager in the hall. 3. She screams with fear.
Solution to the Problem	The manager actually likes dogs, especially big dogs. She says the boy can keep him.

Glossary

collapsed   (kuh-LAPST) fell to the ground (page 8)

concerned   (kun-SERND) worried (page 7)

crabby   (KRA-bee) grumpy (page 15)

drooping   (DROO-ping) sagging (page 18)

filth   (FILTH) dirt (page 18)

gigantic   (jy-GAN-tik) very large (page 19)

hollering   (HAH-luh-ring) yelling (page 8)

murmuring   (MER-muh-ring) low muttering (page 9)

panting   (PAN-ting) breathing loudly (page 11)

skidding   (SKIH-ding) sliding sideways (page 19)